Carrie Stevens Walter

An Idyl of Santa Barbara

Carrie Stevens Walter

An Idyl of Santa Barbara

ISBN/EAN: 9783337378035

Printed in Europe, USA, Canada, Australia, Japan

Cover: Foto ©Andreas Hilbeck / pixelio.de

More available books at **www.hansebooks.com**

AN IDYL

OF

Santa * Barbara.

A fragmentary tale
Half told and half inferred,
As full of sighs and heartache tones
As song of prisoned bird.

CARRIE STEVENS WALTER.

SAN FRANCISCO:
GOLDEN ERA COMPANY, 420 MONTGOMERY ST.
1886.

TO

MY CHILDREN,

WILLIAM, MARY, ROY & DELLA,

Whose loving faith has been my inspiration,

and my life's anchor, this little

brain waif is lovingly

dedicated,

NIGHTFALL AT SANTA BARBARA.

A precious amber vase just filled from elysian fountains
   Whose sacred libation is poured to the year's expiring ember,—
A chalice whose wine is spilled over ocean and islands and mountains—
   Is the close of this perfect day of our California December.

Like ghosts of the Past stand the towers, cross-tipped, of the Church of the Mission,
   While closer and closer the shadows creep round them like stricken things;
The shadows—that seem like the souls of the years that have bowed at its altar,
   Or like land birds blown out over ocean, that droop their desolate wings.

An Idyl of Santa Barbara.

PART I.

Where the roses' rich gifts are completest,
Where sea-winds kiss odorous trees,
Where Song's liquid numbers are sweetest,
Santa Barbara looks out o'er the seas.

HERE are the letters, just as they were put away almost twenty years ago, yellowed by time,—the blue cord that held them, faded and worn. There is no reason to withhold their contents now, for the hearts whose pulse-beats their faded characters chronicled, are stilled forever.

A slender shaft at Lone Mountain, beneath which rests the fair golden head of her who was dearer to me than a sister; a cross-marked grave in Spain, that lies adjacent to a famous cholera hospital within the walls of which a noble life was nobly ended in the cause of suffering humanity,—these will not be affected if I tell the story of the letters.

Memory takes me back over the years that are gone, to the day I saw her last—my dearest friend, Agnes Lee. Her image is before

me as vividly to-day as it was the day I bade her "good-bye" on
the Santa Barbara steamer that carried her from me forever. She
went to spend a year in that southern city ; before the year had
passed, I was called suddenly to my eastern home, and we never
met again. Let me shut my eyes and recall her image as she
stood on the deck of the old *Orizaba* ; her slender form outlined
against the background of wave and sky ; her gracefully poised head
with its mass of golden hair ; the luminous grey eyes, that were
fitting windows of the pure, noble soul within ; the tender, sensitive
mouth that must have love or suffer ; the delicate hands that
clasped those of her two children, Paul and Mary, as though they
were the anchors of her life—as they were. A pure, true woman,
capable of deep feeling, of happiness, or suffering.

In her early girlhood she had married Captain Lee. I could
never understand why she did so. It was one of those incongruous
unions that we see sometimes, the sight of which gives one the heartache. He was a stern, cold, undemonstrative man, born to com-
mand, recognizing no course of conduct from those around him but
obedience to his will. Agnes' nature was such that she would be a
faithful, dutiful wife, under almost any circumstances ; yet there were
moments when I fancied I detected faint scintillations of a Vesuvius
in her soul, of which she was utterly unconscious,—poor child ! And
I trembled lest she should encounter in her life journey an electric
force that would break the seals of her soul's deepest fountains.
Then—God help her !

Two living children, and a little grave at Lone Mountain—these
were the fruits of the twelve years of her married life.

And now, during his absence in China, Captain Lee was sending

Agnes and the two children to Santa Barbara. She was never very robust, and the climate would benefit her. She was devoted to art, and her brush and pencil would find ample scope for their most inspired expressions in this lovely region.

And thus we parted, she, with many regrets that I could not share her journey, with many promises to write me, almost daily, in the form of a journal, her impressions of the scenery and people; and I, with a keen foreboding, only too sadly realized, that our parting was forever.

And now, I will let her letters and journal tell the story. I open the first :

"SANTA BARBARA, June 1, 18—

"MY DEAREST FRIEND : 'Oh ! what is so rare as a day in June ? ' I never realized the full meaning of that line until I came here. I wish I could photograph this lovely scene upon your vision, Kate, and make you so enamored of its witchery that you would desert the bleaker North for this warm, delicious South. We anchored—yes, literally *anchored*—in Santa Barbara harbor last Sunday, about four o'clock in the afternoon. So lovely a crescent of soft, undulating waters, imprisoning, in its ardent embrace, such glorious lights and shades, caught from the admiring sky overhead, and all framed in such greenness of landscape, such golden brownness of hills, over which palpitates, as a living presence, the warm, magnetic atmosphere —all these surely are not found anywhere else upon the earth. Paul and Mary were fairly wild with enjoyment, which culminated when a dear little row-boat was let down from the steamer's side, and we took our seats in it to go on shore.

"After rowing about a mile we landed on a wharf extending a few rods from the shore, and found carriages waiting to convey us to the city proper. The sun was just setting as we drove up State street, and the whole warm, delicious atmosphere was luminous with the rich caressing radiance so peculiar to the southern climate. State street is a broad avenue on each side of which are great, roomy, private mansions with their wide corridors and open windows, half hidden by roses and pepper trees. This latter is the most graceful thing I ever saw in the form of a tree, with its dainty, lace-like foliage, and its true home is in the south.

"The people were all on the streets, I imagine, enjoying the loveliness of the evening. As we drove through its length we observed them with interest. You know the inhabitants are mostly Spanish and native Californians. The ladies were bare-headed, or wore only lace shawls over their heads, put on in that inimitable manner peculiar to the Spanish women, who are always graceful, and always attractive—to *me.*

"At many doors were seated groups, from which almost invariably came the sound of the guitar accompanying some Spanish song. The Spanish song is almost always an ardent, passionate appeal, half religion and all love, and I think some of the airs the most syren-like I ever heard. The atmosphere is always rich with the odor of roses and other fragrant blossoms, the sound of music is seldom stilled ; the nights are lovelier than one can imagine who has never been in the South—and, dear, I believe we will be very happy and contented here. We are to live in the family of Don Ramon Carillo, an old friend of Captian Lee. The family consists of eight children, besides an unlimited number of cousins and other relatives, to the forty-first remove—for they believe in ties of blood, these warm-hearted, hospitable people. These, with a large retinue of servants, make quite a community in itself.

"The house was an old-fashioned *adobe*, originally, but has been remodeled somewhat after a more modern fashion. The rooms are immense. Let me describe them to you. On the first floor are all the living rooms, including a large room for dancing and evening amusements, furnished with two pianos, besides any number of guitars and other musical instruments.

"The floors are all guiltless of that abomination of civilization, the filth-harboring woolen carpet; but the painted floors are as clean as they can be, and soft rugs and mats are thrown down wherever they can do the most good. Our sleeping rooms are on the second floor, and are great, wide, airy apartments that are delightfully comfortable. Mine contains a large bed, and two small ones for the children; and it has, oh! I don't know how many windows opening upon the corridor outside. We have only to step outside of our room to reach the loveliest climbing roses you ever saw,—great, golden-hearted, satin-petaled masses of fragrance and beauty that give me exquisite pleasure. We have roses in unlimited quantities in our room all the time, for Anita, the maid who has the care of it, knows my passion for flowers, and together with the children, keeps the vases always freshly filled. And the children—I wish you could see their enjoyment! The only thing to mar their perfect bliss is the fact that figs and grapes are not ripe yet. Yes—let me repeat my former assertion—I believe we shall be very happy and contented here.

"JUNE 6th.

"If I were a *man*, Kate, I should certainly fall deliberately in love with Rose Carillo, who is the loveliest creature 'I ever saw. She is Don Ramon's eldest daughter, and his idol, of course. She is in her nineteenth year, and it would seem that Southern beauty and grace had found their personification in her. Tall, with a form exquisitely molded, every motion of which is grace, her face a dainty oval, with that rich, olive complexion peculiar to her race— for Don Ramon is a native of old Castile—her hair a luxuriant mass of satin blackness, that falls almost to her feet when she stands erect. But her eyes—great, wondrous orbs, that melt or burn as the mood of the spirit behind them prompts—these are her chief glory. She is a queen, an empress, among women.

How attractive these dark people are to me! I presume it is always the case with us red-haired sensitives. I think I was first attracted to you, Kate, because you are so delightfully brown.

"Don Ramon is a courtly Spanish gentleman of the old school; his wife, the Doña Inez, is a sweet, gentle, motherly soul, who pets and cuddles her children, worships her husband, and fulfills all her duties according to the standard of her race. The children are a happy lot of lads and lasses, all pretty, and all lovingly devoted to 'papa' and 'mama' and each other. Rose and her father speak English perfectly; in fact, Rose has been well educated, having passed some time at school in San Francisco. Doña Inez does not speak English at all, and the children only slightly; so you see I shall be compelled to brush up the Spanish lessons of my schooldays. I believe I can conquer the musical cadences of the language in a short time, as Rose has taken me in hand as a pupil, and I am to give her lessons in painting.

"JUNE 12TH.

"But a genuine Spanish *baile*, Kate, is a most delightful affair. Yesterday was Rose's birthday, and Don Ramon made a party in her honor. The true Spaniard takes time for enjoyment, and has no patience with us hard-working Yankees.

"The great dancing room was one garden of flowers. The Santa Barbara band, composed entirely of native Californians, was ordered for the occasion; and for a day or two, troops of servants were running hither and yon, preparing the banquet for the evening. Gay lanterns were distributed through the grounds, for the promenading and chatting between dances were to be done out of doors to a great extent. In one corner of the room was a little marble stand on which were placed several baskets containing egg shells, from which the contents had been carefully removed, and the shells filled with gilt and various colored paper cut as fine as possible. These were great mysteries to Paul and Mary, who waited with much curiosity until evening, to see of what possible use *egg shells* could be at a party.

"There was a large company of the very *elite* of the Spanish society, together with several American families. There were many pretty girls, but my gorgeous Rose surpassed them all, as much as her name-flower surpasses the field poppy. She was resplendent in a dress of pale pink silk. Her eyes were luminous as suns. Through all the mazes of the graceful Spanish quadrille she seemed the embodiment of the poetry of motion. My delight was in watching her throughout the evening. She has conceived a warm attachment for me, and playfully calls me her 'Saint Agnes,' or as she often puts it, *'Santita mia.'*

"The dancing continues at a Spanish *baile*, until the dancers become weary, then all rest for half an hour or longer, occupying the time in chatting, singing or promenading. At such intervals we saw the use of those mysterious egg-shells—*cascarones*, as they are called in Spanish. A gentleman desires to express his admiration for a lady, or compliment her; he, therefore, takes one of these *cascarones* and breaks it over her head, the minced paper falling in a rainbow shower over her hair. The belles of the evening thus presented a very parti-colored appearance before the *baile* was over. Paul and Mary were immensely amused with all they saw. They are beginning to say many words in Spanish, and I doubt not, will learn to speak the language before our year is ended.

"But I am worried about Rose, dear. Perhaps I am foolish, but I feel anxious in spite of myself. A frequent caller at the house is a lawyer by the name of Charles Howard. He is Don Ramon's legal adviser, and, therefore, has a good reason for his calls, as business is nearly always the excuse. He is a man of perhaps thirty years of age, who some ten years ago was drawn into a marriage with a woman much older than himself. She is not his equal intellectually, and I do not imagine their married life is of the most loving sort. He is one of those golden haired Apollos, that my dark-eyed Rose would fancy in spite of herself. He danced with her several times last night, and I fancied I saw a brighter look in her eyes, and a richer color on her cheeks when she was with him. I wish he would keep away from her.

"He has two pretty little children to whom he is devotedly attached. His wife is a good mother, it is said,—and I don't see why he cannot stay at home with his family. However, his wife and children were present last evening. I don't like her. She is a small, common nature,—and—oh! dear, I don't know what I dread. But he is a very attractive man, of superior intelligence, and a thorough gentleman in every particular of manner and speech.

"Maybe I'm tired and nervous to-night. I guess I'll go to bed and sleep off my fears. Rose has just come in for a moment's good-night chat. She takes my face between her hands, turns it up to her while she kisses me and says, '*Buena noche, Santita mia*, you are tired ; sleep as late as possible to-morrow morning ;'—and I will.

"Good night, darling.

"YOUR AGNES."

PART II.

Among the silver threads of Life,
So closely twine Love's golden strands,
That when we loose their clinging hold,
The fabric crumbles in our hands.

"SANTA BARBARA, July 5th.

E celebrated 'our glorious Independence,' yesterday, with a picnic down the coast. I wish you could have been with us, dear. There were few beside the members of Don Ramon's family. By the way, there have been two additions to our family circle within the past few days, of whom I must tell you. The first under consideration is Colonel Horton, an old acquaintance of Captain Lee. I believe he has been in several Indian campaigns, and is quite a hero in the eyes of civilians. He has a tall, military figure, and the manners of a king ; commanding, yet polished and courteous. His black hair, and heavy, dark moustache are sprinkled with gray, while his deep gray eyes are shaded by heavy, black brows. He has one of those firm, square chins that always indicate strength of character, and there is something about the man that interests one.

"The other person is a brother of Don Ramon, who has lately come from Spain. He, also, is quite a character. For many years he was one of the leading physicians of Madrid, and in the pursuit of his profession was brought in contact with nearly every form of suffering humanity. His whole energies were given to his work, and to the relief of the afflicted. He seemed so impressed with the idea of working solely for humanity, that, a few years ago, he took holy orders, and was ordained a priest, devoting his life to the work of aiding the afflicted, not only as a physician, but in other ways. All this Rose told me of him before I met him, so you may imagine I watched him with some interest.

"Father Antonio, as he is called, is rather below the medium in height, with the olive complexion peculiar to his race. His dark eyes are singularly expressive, varying with his mood in a fashion peculiarly characteristic. They flashed like flames the other day, at some tale of wrong and outrage, and I thought I should always stand in awe of their owner. Yet, soon afterwards, a little child of our party fell on the rocks, and was badly hurt; Father Antonio sprang to her assistance at once, and while aiding him to relieve her pain, I accidentally encountered his glance. I do not think I ever before saw an expression of such sweetness and tenderness in human eyes. He seems singularly self-forgetful, yet is rather reserved and reticent in a manner that gives one the impression of haughtiness.

"Well! Kate, how I have gossiped about our new-comers! I know you will smile at my letter. But, remember, our life is so quiet here, that even trifling incidents assume proportions of importance. This must be my excuse.

"We went down the Coast in carriages as far as Rincon Point, where there is a stage station. Then fires were built and we had a clam-bake,—all of which was very pleasant. The children enjoyed the bliss of running through the waves with bare feet, which, of course, is a new experience to Paul and Mary. They are becoming regular little Spaniards. It would amuse you to hear them chatter the language. They say nothing in English that they can possibly twist into this musical idiom.

"This life is very restful and pleasant to me, Kate. It seems a leaf from Bohemia, and I dread the thought of ever returning to a practical, matter-of-fact existence again. Did I tell you Mr. Howard, that lawyer I mentioned before, was of our picnic party? He came out on horseback after we had arrived at the grounds. I watched him closely. I don't know what he means by keeping with Rose so much. I do not like it; and yet, somehow, I feel that he is not a dishonorable man. And Rose,—dear girl—I watched her every glance and expression jealously, and I feel that she is much interested in him, more than she realizes. I want to snatch her in my arms and run away with her. She had her guitar with her, to which she sings divinely these bewildering Spanish songs. One, whose air is the most impassioned I ever heard, she has promised to put into English for me some time. There is something in these Spanish songs, with the guitar accompaniment, that arouses all the instincts of the tropics in one's nature; they draw my heart through my eyes, in tears, and I want to run away from myself.

"Rose has just come to my door, and in her pretty liquid tones called to me '*Santita*, we are going to take you on a famous trip to-morrow. We are all going up in the hills beyond the town, on horseback, and you can make some lovely sketches while we are resting. You know we *Espanoles* never forget to rest when it is nec_essary.'

"I reply, 'What, Rose, *all* of you? Do you mean your mother and all the *muchachitos?*'

"'What nonsense!' she replies, laughing; 'I mean papa, Col. Horton, Uncle Antonio, you and I, and I believe papa has invited Mr. Howard to be of the party.' This latter clause was spoken with a hightened color, which my keen glance did not tend to relieve.

"July 25th.

"How good these people are to me, Kate! Each seems to vie with the other in making my life 'as pleasant as possible. I seem to live in a dream of southern glory. Sunshine, brighter than you have ever seen in your northern home; the beauty and fragrance of ever-blooming flowers; music, almost without cessation ; and moonlight nights that remind one of the vale of Cashmere—isn't that a list of attractions to arouse your envy? Our life has been a constant routine of walks, drives, or horseback rides during the past three weeks, and we have all become wonderfully good friends during these days in which the conventionalities have been somewhat ignored. For you know, one cannot take the strictest rules of etiquette into the woods, or sailing on the water, when the waves are liable to give him a playful wetting. Father Antonio occasionally accompanies us, but he is much occupied during the day, and does not often join our circle until evening. Col. Horton is very kind and thoughtful. His acquaintance with Captain Lee gives him the privileges of an old friend to me and the children.

And yet, I have come away from the happy party down stairs, to-night, dear friend, to commune with you, because my heart is so full of memories that I shall suffocate unless I feel the clasp of your spirit-hand a little while, and the benediction of your love. You know this is the anniversary of my baby's death, and also of my marriage. Oh ! my precious baby ! Must I wait until I put off this weary thralldom of the flesh before I can again hold his beloved form to my heart, or feel the caressing of his little hands? Kate, Kate ! I'm all at sea to-night. As I pace the long room like a caged animal, I feel that there is much of the caged animal in my nature. I'm afraid of myself. I want to talk to you to-night as I never yet have spoken to any one, and as I could speak to no one but *you ;* for in all my life, since I have known you,

* * * ' I never turned round and missed *you*
From my side in one hour of affliction or doubt.'

I know, in the genuine battles of life, there is no help for us from any source but the Divine. Those who love us can only stand by and pray for us in the greatest extremities of our lives. You have guessed without my telling, that away back in the days of romantic girlhood, I staked all in life upon the hope of love and kindness and domestic happiness. I do not believe in the doctrine of mistakes, else I might use the term in connection with my life. Destiny had other uses for me, I presume, that were inconsistent with the gratification of the strong woman nature that demanded so much. The highest standard of life is *duty*. I know those four letters are seared upon my heart. I only ask God and his angels to help me to perform my whole duty unflinchingly to the happy end of life.

" Dear, love meant so much to me that was high, pure and divine
The ideal reached the clouds—no, not clouds, but beyond the clouds
into the heavenly ether. That ideal I cling to as my salvation
There is, in some far distant stage of existence, the realization of our

grandest ideals, else creation were a lie. Whatever may be the
design of these long years of starvation, I believe the whole plan is
right and good. I also believe that some day, in another life·—*never
in this*—I shall encounter the grand nature that only can realize the
ideal.

"There is no such reality here. I live for that far distant time,
and in the intervening ages in which I am becoming worthy of that
hour, I pray for strength to do nothing that may mar or retard the
completeness of it. I know there is in my nature a depth that can
never be fathomed here ; I know this perfectly, therefore I walk in
armor. And yet I come back to what I said in the beginning, 'I
am afraid of myself at times.' Pray for me, dear girl ; I know it
will aid me. Forgive this wild letter, and do not misunderstand me ;
you never did. Your faith and love are my refuge, Kate—Good
night.

"AUGUST 8th.

" Such trouble as I have been having with Rose ! I don't know
what I am going to do with the dear girl, more than to try my best to
hold her firmly in the right course. I will tell you the whole story.
Yesterday afternoon I was alone in the sitting-room, finishing a sketch
from memory that I had taken of the old Mission Church. For
some reason there was no one else at home but Rose and the servants.
I was working with no thought on anything but my work, when she
came into the room and stood beside me, with one arm thrown around
me. Finally she spoke with hesitation, half playfully :

" ' *Santita*, you remember I promised you a translation of that
song, the air of which you like so well. " *Un adios*," it is called,
only I have re-christened it "Tempest-Tossed." ' '

"'Yes,' I replied, interestedly, putting down my brush ; 'I am very anxious to hear the words of that song. The air thrills me so strangely that I am sure the words must have some hidden power, also. I am not sufficiently advanced in my Spanish studies to be able to get the real meaning of the poetry. Have you translated your "Tempest-Tossed" for me, Rose?'

"'*Si, hermanita*,—wasn't I industrious to do so when you know I don't like work? But this is just for *you* alone, and I do not want any one else to see it.'

"There was something nervous and constrained in her manner, although she tried to seem careless and indifferent, as she handed me a folded paper.

"'Oh! Rose, I am tired,' I said ; 'can you not complete your kindness by reading the song to me? I shall appreciate it much more.'

"'Why, yes, dear; if you wish it very much,' and she took a foot-stool at my feet, while I leaned back in my easy chair and watched her. My heart was filled with admiration and love for the beautiful girl, and I was thinking more of her, than of her reading, when something in the words arrested my attention, and I listened with a great heartache for her. But let me give you the impassioned verses, just as she read them in her low, musical fashion, trembling and hesitating sometimes, but reading to the close. This is the song :

TEMPEST TOSSED.

What does it mean, this tyrant spell that holds me
A captive in its chains ;
That thrills my wayward heart with strong emotion,—
Love's passion,—and its pains?

Oh, restless soul ! that beats Life's bars unceasing,—
    A tiger held in thrall !
Oh, passion's surge ! that would engulf calm reason
    And give to Love Life's all.

Can I not curb the strong, defiant feeling
    That struggles in my soul,
And scorns all forms and laws that cold convention
    Would frame in Love's control ?

I strive—in vain ; for all that Life could grant me,
    Or Hope's bright vision greet,
My passionate heart would,—haughty as an empress,—
    Fling proudly at your feet,

And ask no gift from you in compensation,
    No love-thrill in return.
My own—unsought—from Life's rich depths must greet me,
    All else my heart must spurn.

I bear no thought of shame for this strong passion
    Of my best womanhood ;
Love bears God's seal, and its divine·expression
    Is always pure and good.

You are to me the noblest realization
    Of manhood, grand and true,
The one man in God's universe.   I care not
    What I may be to you.

And thus—to live—swayed by a god-like passion,
    That may not be expressed ;
To bravely strive,—yet never quite subduing
    Love's longing and unrest.

"She read the last words almost in a whisper, and I could feel her form shiver, as she leaned against me.

"'Rose! Rose!' I said, with a feeling of agony that must have expressed itself in my voice, 'never sing that song again, or *think* of it! You must not! Oh, my poor child! you are tottering on a fearful brink!'

"She bowed her head in my lap, trembling visibly, as she replied:

"'Sister Agnes, I am no longer on the brink. I am in the great, deep abyss, God help me! I *love him* as only one of my nature and my race can love. I do not think he gives me a moment's thought; he does not care for me, why should he? I do not want to *desire* his love. He is all that is honorable and good; and yet, I am conscious of only this, in every fiber of my soul and body, *I love him, I love him!*

"Hush! Rose,' I cried, 'hush! remember what he is—the husband of another woman.'

"'As if I could ever forget it!' she replied passionately. 'Sister Agnes, the nature of a Spanish woman can no more be held in the grooves of propriety and conventionalism than a mountain torrent. God made me as I am, and He knows I am not to blame for loving *the husband of another woman.*'

"'No, dear child,' I said, taking both her little, hot hands in mine; 'you are not to blame for that, but you are very much to blame, if by one act or word, you do aught that could give one pang to that *other woman*, were she the most loving and sensitive of wives.'

"'Agnes, can you doubt me? I do not propose to do anything —but feel and suffer. You do not understand my nature. How can one of your cold Northern blood understand our Southern intensity? Charles Howard is the soul of honor. He would die before he could do a dishonorable act. And I? Why Agnes !' her low, impassioned tones were like music as she spoke, 'it is no idle expression when I say that I would give my life for his happiness, or his good, as readily as I give you a rose ; and yet so proud am I that I would not by one wave of my hand call him to my side, unless he came first of his own free will. There is no sacrifice I would not make for him ; yet I would not cross this room to win him, were he entirely free, unless I knew that I am to him what he is to me. With this knowledge in my heart, and no bonds of honor to bind me, there is no place in God's universe where I would not go to him. There is no chasm my love could not bridge, no heights or depths it would not pierce, to bring me to his side—his equal, his queen.'

"She had risen in speaking, and was standing before me like a goddess ; the glory of the heavens was shining in her eyes, and the strength of her emotion seemed to exalt her before me. I raised my eyes to reply to her, when there before me, in one of the long, open French windows, stood Charles Howard. His face was pale as marble, and the light in his eyes made me think of an eruption of Vesuvius I once witnessed. Rose stood with her back to him, and was unconscious of his presence. I knew he had heard her last words, and perhaps more. I felt myself getting faint and dizzy at the situation ; but was prevented making any movement in the matter by Howard, who did not notice me at all, but came towards Rose with both arms held out, exclaiming, with a passionate ring in his voice :

"'Then come to me, *my darling!* God knows the best love of your glorious nature can be but a response to what I have felt for you since I first knew you.'

"Rose turned, and instantly the proud look and carriage were gone. She was simply the loving woman, who, with a low cry, sprang into his arms, where he held her as though he intended that nothing should ever separate them again.

"For a 'moment I was so overcome by this terrible complication of affairs, that I felt weak enough to run away and never come back again. Then the whole magnitude of their danger seemed to rise up before me and invest me with personal responsibility in this matter, and to give me strength beyond myself. I went to them, took Rose from him and held her closely in my arms while I said, with a force that arrested his attention :

"'Mr. Howard, are you insane? Do you stop one moment to consider the full meaning of your words and act? Would you blast the life of this precious girl?'

"'Mrs. Lee,' he replied, with a dignity that won my respect, 'you misunderstand my motives. I would not allow a breath to mar the purity of her fame, which is more sacred to me than anything in earth or heaven. God knows you would seem to have a right to judge me harshly, but I never intended to let Rose know my feelings for her. I know that every instinct of honor and principle would seem to forbid it. This betrayal of my true self was unintentional. But knowing what I do *now*, I shall have but one aim in life henceforth, to make the way plain and straight to put myself in a position where I can claim her before the world. Until then I shall not allow myself the bliss of even clasping her hand or meeting her dear eyes. If you knew the whole story of my life, Mrs. Lee, you would not blame me as I feel you do. Sometime you may know more of me. I know you love Rose, as she does you. Will you not try to have faith in me, and believe that I am an honorable man, a proud man who holds himself above the contamination of the mire of sensuality? I will prove it to you and I will claim my darling one day in a manner that even *you* will approve.'

"His tone and manner were so manly that somehow, despite myself, I found that I *did* have faith in his expressions.

" 'Mr. Howard,' I said as frankly as I felt, 'I have faith in you now. I believe you mean just what you say. But humanity is weak. You must go beyond the reach of temptation at once. I, of course know nothing of your life story, but I feel an interest in you, and shall pray that these tangled threads may all be made straight. I love Rose as my own younger sister. Her welfare is as precious to me as that of my own little daughter.'

" 'I am glad it is so,' she replied; 'I had already made arrangements to go away to Santa Barbara for an indefinite period. I shall now hasten those plans. Let me assure you once more that you shall never have reason to doubt my honor. Before I go away, may I not see you for a few moments? There is much I would say to you, if you will hear it.'

"I gave him the desired promise. I was getting very nervous lest some other members of the family, should return and guess by our appearance that something unusual had occurred. Then I hastened his departure and took Rose off to my room just in time to avoid observation. Once inside my door and the key safely turned she sank down, faint and weak, and lay sobbing in my arms like a child. I kept her with me all night, giving a nervous headache, that stereotyped excuse, as my reason for doing so. And now, do you wonder at my anxiety? Rose clings to me as her only refuge, and I feel that I must be brave and strong to support her. Write soon, dear Kate, and give me the comfort of some of your strong, good words.

"Your loving AGNES."

PART III.

From the arms held out to embrace us,
  We shrink with a moan, to pray
For the pressure of arms that are folded,
  Forever and ever away.

"SANTA BARBARA, Aug 29th.

HAVE neglected you, Kate, during these sunny
August days; but I have had so much to fill my
mind and heart that I could not write. There
has been a severe epidemic of measles raging
among the children of Santa Barbara for some
weeks. Two of Don Ramon's little ones were
quite ill for several days, having been stricken
with the disease a day or two after my last letter
to you. My own precious lambs are exempt
from the contagion—as you know—you probably
not having forgotten their two weeks' illness a year ago, through
which you helped me to nurse them. Therefore, having no fears for
their welfare to deter me, I have gone much among the little sufferers
of our acquaintance. You know I have a sort of 'gift' in the line of
hospital work, and I remember how you used to say I was never
happier than when fondling some sick baby or soothing the ails of
some old woman.

" Two weeks ago last night, Mrs. Howard sent for me to go to
her, as both her little girls were sick. Charles Howard had been
called suddenly and unexpectedly to San Francisco upon business

and she was alone. You may imagine I was somewhat surprised at the summons, but went at once. She met me at the door saying, ' Excuse me for sending for you, Mrs. Lee, but I am told you know just what to do for sick children, and I am a poor nurse. I know my children are very sick, and I am afraid old Dr. Simmons is not helping them.'

" I went with her to the bedroom where the little girls were tossing and moaning in the delirium of fever. I saw immediately that their condition was serious. Jennie, the elder, who is about nine years of age, seemed in a half stupor which I did not like; but Maude, the younger child, who is near seven, was very restless. A great many bottles with formidable labels and directions stood on a little table. After a few minutes' careful inspection I said :

" ' Mrs. Howard, the little girls *are* very sick. This room is too hot and close. Your sitting-room is cooler and has better ventilation. Can we not arrange two cots there, where the children will be more comfortable ?'

" ' Anything you think best, Mrs. Lee,' she exclaimed. ' I know so little about nursing that I feel helpless in this case Will you not stay with me and advise we what to do ?' I readily gave the desired promise and we soon had two cool, comfortable cots in the pleasant sitting-room to which we carried the little sufferers out of the stifling bedroom. I was not pleased with the amount of drugs prescribed by Dr. Simmons, and earnestly desired to toss the whole array of bottles into the kitchen fire. But you know how one feels about suggesting anything contrary to a physician's directions, even if he is antediluvian in his ideas. Therefore, I remained silent while dose after dose of strong nauseous drugs was poured down each poor little

parched throat. Sad hours of anxious watching followed, broken by
an occasional call from some friendly neighbor, and the regular visits
of the fussy old doctor, who seemed bewildered and uncertain in the
management of the cases. I remained through the night, going home
in the early morning for rest and sleep. As I came in at the gate of
Don Ramon's home I met Father Antonio walking among the roses.
I do not know what there is in that strong, quiet face of his that
inspires me with such a feeling of rest—of refuge in distress. There
is a certain dignity of character, a certain holding himself above the
multitude, that would seem to repel any personal familiarity, and yet
sometimes there flashes over me the feeling that in any terrible emer-
gency, spiritual or physical, I should turn instinctively to him as to
a rock of refuge. In my anxiety for my poor little patients this feeling prompted me to respond to his courteous greeting by giving him
a full account of the symptons and mode of treatment of the sick
children. His face became very serious as he listened, and when I
had finished the recital he paused a moment in thought before
answering :

" ' You are quite right, Mrs. Lee, in your opinion that the little
ones are in danger, more from an incompetent physician than from
the disease. But my dear madame, you are very weary. It is not
right for you to give too much from your fund of vitality, although it
is given in a noble cause. What a fine nurse you are,' he said, smil-
ing. I never noticed before what an amount of sunshine there was
in his smile ; and as I passed into the house, a something from his
personality, as an emanation, seemed to go with me to soothe and
quiet me.

"I slept some hours, and when I awoke, Rose, dear girl, had

brought me a silver tray containing a cup of delicious chocolate and some other refreshments. 'Uncle Antonio says you must take this and when you go back to your patients, he will accompany you,' she said with a little quiver in her voice ; 'Oh, Agnes, do you think there is any danger?' and the tear drops glistened on her long lashes.

' There is danger, dear,' I replied, 'danger in the amount of drugs they are compelled to take. If your Uncle could have had the management of their cases from the beginning the children would have fared no worse than your little brother and sister.' She remained silent while I took my chocolate, then said with a tone of dignity and sweetness :

"'Sister Agnes, I want to aid you in the care of the little sick ones. You must let me relieve you with them. There can be not the least impropriety while their father is away. Oh ! Agnes they are *his* children, and I cannot tell you how it hurts me to think of their suffering. I must help you with them until he comes.'

" I was thoughtful a moment before replying. The children needed just such help as Rose could give them ; there was no reason in the eyes of the community why she should not act a neighborly part to Mrs. Howard. That eventful scene in the parlor, described in my last letter, no one besides ourselves suspected. I believe she would be happier ministering to the needs of the little ones, than to be idle, therefore I replied :

"'You may help me Rose ; there is no reason why you should not.' Then we went down to her uncle, who awaited us on the great wide veranda, and together went to Mrs. Howard's.

" I watched Father Antonio closely, as he examined the little ones, and I did not gather hope from his face.

" It was necessary for the children to have careful attention day and night. The neighbors who had children of their own were fearful of exposing them by coming in to assist Mrs. Howard, and it was impossible to hire the proper kind of nursing, Therefore it devolved upon us to do all we could. The mother looked worn and exhausted from lack of sleep. Father Antonio came to our aid at once in his firm, quiet manner, arranging that he and Rose should watch through the night, and insisting that Mrs. Howard and I should retire, and leave everything to his care. He seemed to take my burden from me in a way that relieved my anxious heart, immensely. It was but a short distance to Don Ramon's and as I thought best to go back to my own darling's instead of remaining at Mrs. Howard's, he accompanied me to the gate, and then returned to Rose, and their vigil.

" ' Through the next day two of the neighbors aided the mother in the care of the children who were no better. In the evening as I was passing out of Don Ramon's gate on my way to Mrs. Howard's I was joined by Father Antonio who remarked ' It is best that I should remain through the night with our invalids. I do not think it wise for you to be alone with them and the mother.'

" Towards midnight the children seemed more quiet, and Father Antonio said to me in a low voice :

" ' Mrs. Lee, insist upon Mrs. Howard taking some refreshment, and then getting some sleep. She will need all her vitality to meet what is coming soon.' I looked at him in a startled way, because I had thought the children improving.

" ' And what of their father ? ' I questioned, anxiously.

" ' His partner has telegraphed him to return at once ; and he responded that he would leave immediately, returning overland.   He is undoubtedly on the road now.'

" I went into the little kitchen where there was a fire, made some tea and toast which I prevailed upon the mother sharing with me. She was weary and unstrung which must account, in part, for the singular confidences upon her part which followed. She is a peculiar woman; I am not attracted to her, and yet I pity her. She is dark and sallow in appearance, and looks much older than her husband. Her abundant black hair is coiled at the back of her head, usually in a manner that gives her a sort of witch-like appearance, and there is a peculiar glitter in her small, black eyes that does not tend to lessen this impression. She has one of those long, pointed chins, and the mouth which usually accompanies it, giving a shrewish appearance to the face. Yet she has been a pretty girl, and is a model house-keeper ;—but I never liked *model house-keepers*. Their realm is generally the kingdom of small things, and they are more troubled about much serving, and the infinitesimals of existence than anything of a broader nature.

" As we sat by the kitchen table drinking our tea, she suddenly broke into a passion of sobs. I attempted to soothe her, and in a few moments she became more calm, saying :

"' Mrs. Lee, you have been so good to me, I want to talk to you to-night about something I have never mentioned in California.'

"I told her I should be glad to do her any good in my power by sympathy or otherwise. Then followed this singular recital, which was all the more surprising, following the strange events of the past few weeks.

"' I believe my children are going to die, Mrs. Lee. I feel that it will be God's punishment to me for some things of my past life, which weigh upon me so heavily to-night, that I must tell you of them to ease my heart.

"'About twelve years ago I was living in my father's home in one of the interior towns of New York. I had been something of a belle in my girlhood, and then, at twenty-eight had much attention, for my gayety of manner and vivacity, I presume, as much as for my father's wealth. But I had never thought seriously about marriage, or met one whom I cared for in that way, until the time I speak of. There came to our town, partly upon business and partly for recreation, a gentleman from New Orleans named Victor Ellerton. He was a genuine Southerner of the noblest sort, so I thought, handsome, chivalrous and manly. He was two or three years my senior, and, from the hour I met him, I loved him as I never loved before, or since. He was the one idol of my wayward heart, and my stubborn will was completely conquered. He was attentive to me, in fact, conspicuously so, and I was happy. But you will see by what I tell you, that my happiness excited the jealousy and malice of a young girl of the place, Julia Gregory, who had boldly tried to win his attention from the first. One day he came to me much agitated, saying he had just received a telegram of his mother's illness, and was compelled to return at once to New Orleans. There were several persons present at his call, but as I accompanied him to the door, and stood a moment with him, he took my hand in his, and said in a low tone, "Miss Wilson—*Jennie* may I call you?—I have so much I want to tell you. May I write to you?" As I gave the permission, I know my face betrayed my love for him. I looked forward with happy anticipations to the coming of the expected letter. Every day I went to the postoffice, but it never came. I cannot tell the feelings I endured as the long summer passed and no word came from him. Then malicious persons began to whisper that I had been jilted, and my irritation was at its height, when one day as I called at the postoffice, Julia Gregory, whose father was postmaster, handed me a New Orleans paper with a marked paragraph, remarking :

"'And so, Jennie, our Southerner was a gay deceiver after all, wasn't he? But you and I don't care, do we? We know there is just as good fish in the sea.'

"'I took the paper and read the marriage of Victor Ellerton to Alice Irwin, of New Orleans. I went home with rage in my soul. I determined to let everybody see I was not a victim. Charles Howard was a wealthy young law student, who had come from New York City to spend the summer, and had seemed somewhat attentive to me in a bashful, boyish fashion. He was about twenty years of age at that time, and I knew, as women do, sometimes, that if I exerted all my power, I could ensnare his boyish heart, marry him and leave the place—now so hateful to me. Well, I carried out my plans completely. Mrs. Lee, I *entrapped* him into that marriage,—that is just what I did. I do not believe he ever loved me. I hope he has not ; for I have never loved him. My two little girls were born within two years of each other. When Maude was two months old, we determined to come to California. We were then in New York City. I was sitting in my room holding the baby one evening, when the doorbell rang, and a woman asked to see me. It was Mrs. Gregory, Julia's mother, dressed in deep mourning. She told me something that nearly froze the blood in my heart. It was simply this : Victor

Ellerton *had* written to me, as he promised, again and again, but Julia, while acting as her father's assistant, had stolen the letters, and not daring to destroy them, had hidden them. At last she wrote an anonymous letter to Ellerton, telling him I was false to him, and was to marry another. The marriage notice she gave me to read was that of his cousin of the same name. He had never married. Julia had died a month before her mother's visit, and during her last sickness had confessed everything to her mother, asking her to find me and obtain my forgiveness. At the end of the story she gave me the package of sealed letters—his letters, written nearly four years before.

"'Oh! Mrs. Lee, I cannot tell you what I suffered. At first I could not forgive Julia. I nearly broke her poor mother's heart with my angry words. But before she left me I was calmer, and promised to try to forgive her. Then, I went to my room and read those letters. The first told me of his love, and asked me to be his wife. The others were filled with eager inquiries of my silence, and the last bade me farewell, as he had heard of my intended marriage. How I hated my folly, and my weak revengeful nature, that had not only caused me to sacrifice Charles Howard, but had placed a bar between me and the only man I loved. I shed bitter tears over those letters, and when Charles came home that evening, I was honest enough to confess everything to him, and give them to him to read. I supposed he would leave me at once. I should have done so, had I been in his place. But he read them all through ; then, putting his hand on my head, like a brother might have done, said :

"'Poor Jennie ! I am so sorry for you. I read your heart's history long ago. If I could make you happy by leaving you, I should do so. But you need my care and protection to raise our little girls, and for the present it is better for us to remain before the world as we are. When our separation is necessary for your happiness, then we will consider it. I do not blame you, or feel harshly towards you; never think so one moment. But, this I do feel, that we are not in the true sense husband and wife. Let us not degrade that holiest of all relationships by falsehood of word or act. We will offer no sacrifice to false god. Henceforth, you may confide in me as a sister, and I will be a brother to you.'

"'Since that day we have been husband and wife only in name. He is always thoughtful and kind to me, and one of the best of fathers. The children he loves more intensely, I believe from having missed the other love from his life.'

"You can imagine, Kate, with what feelings I heard this story. I wondered if this selfish nature, that was so willing to accept the strangely unselfish sacrifice from the man whose name she bore, could ever rise to the height of being noble and generous in turn, did she know the true condition of affairs. I doubt it. But, perhaps, I do her injustice.

"I persuaded her to retire to her room, and I rejoined Father Antonio in his watching.

"Silently we sat together through the mysterious hours of dying night and coming dawn. It was evident that Jennie could not survive the day. Maude might possibly get well, but we dared not hope too much. With the first flush of daylight Rose came in at the gateway, seeming the spirit of the dawn, in her gown of palest pink. Her eyes were heavy, and she looked pale and anxious. As she came to the side of little Jennie, the child opened her eyes, and whispered in a half-dream like way:

" ' My papa,—I want my dear papa ! '

" Father Antonio put his hand on her head and assured her that her papa was coming to her soon. At this moment the mother came into the room. In an instant she perceived the fatal change in the little girl, and sinking into a chair by the side of the bed broke into a passion of sobs. Father Antonio urged self-control for the sake of the child. Rose stood by the little one with a goblet of water, moistening the parched mouth occasionally as she struggled with the parting breath. Raising her dim eyes to Rose she whispered, 'Take me up, Miss Rose.' The request was instantly obeyed, and the dying child was held carefully in the loving arms, while the little head was pillowed on the tender, womanly breast of Rose. I stood beside the stricken mother, who buried her face in my garments in an agony of weeping.

" ' Papa,' came faintly from the lips around which the grey shadows were creeping.

" At this moment down the silent street came the rapid whirl of wheels and a dust-covered buggy—drawn by two foaming, quivering horses—stopped at the gate. Howard's partner, Mr. James, had met the stage twenty miles from Santa Barbara with the swiftest horses he could secure, and in this way brought the father to his dying child.

" Howard, pale and haggard, sprang from the vehicle and came to the door. Father Antonio met him with a silent hand-clasp. Not a word was spoken as the father sank on his knees by the bedside.

" ' Oh, my baby !' he sobbed. The sobs of a man ! Surely the most agonizing sound that can be voiced.

" ' Papa !' came from the little one, and there was a glad quiver in the weak voice, and a faint light in the rapidly glazing eyes. Rose's face was like that of a marble statue, as she held the little form tenderly, while her beautiful eyes held a passion of agony in their depths.

"Slowly and yet more slowly came the breath of the little girl, the intervals between the faint sighs becoming longer. Lower and lower drooped the lids over the pretty blue eyes. A faint flutter of the breath as a newly awakened bird, and I whispered :

"'She is gone !'—But no, the lids raised, the eyes turned first to the kneeling father, then to the mother, lastly toward heaven, and opened with a glad joyous light. One little hand fell into Rose's clasp, the other fluttered like a rose petal into the hand of her father. The clock on the mantle chimed five. With that bright look in her eyes, with the little hands as they fell, she was gone, and just the wee shell of mortality that once enfolded her, was left to us.

" For some moments the silence was broken only by the sobs of the mother, whose face was buried in my arms. Then, Father Antonio reverently and tenderly lifted the lifeless form from Rose's arms, and placed it on the couch, then, taking Rose's hand, led her quietly away, while I drew the weeping mother into an adjoining room. The father, after passionately kissing the little still face, passed to the bedside of the other child, who was lying in a half-conscious condition at the farther side of the room, carefully attended by a neighbor who had come in soon after his arrival.

" But why prolong the sorrowful details. Little Maude lived until midnight, when she joined her sister. Side by side the little white-robed sisters lay in their coffin, as though they had lain down in their bed at night. I was with the father and mother until the last.

" And now Mrs. Howard will go to her New York home for rest
and change. Charles Howard will remove his business to San
Francisco, and the double grave at the Santa Barbara cemetery will
remain to them as a sacred memory forevermore. Oh, Life ! some
of thy details are stranger than fiction !

" I am very tired, dear, from the events of the past weeks. I am
resting all I can. Col. Horton has returned from a two weeks' business trip to San Buena Ventura and the valley of the Santa Clara.
He is very kind and thoughtful of my comfort, and is constantly
arranging pleasant things for me. They are all so good to me here.

"I see very little of Father Antonio now, as he is much occupied.
Yet, somehow, at any hour I can close my eyes, and see his strong,
refined face, and the vision strengthens me. It is a mysterious
thing, this power of one soul over another.

"You will perceive I have been two or three days writing this
letter. What a blessing you are to me, Kate, my refuge in perplexity
and sorrow.   Lovingly,
                                                            "Agnes."

                                              "SEPTEMBER 3RD.

" Fate is dealing queerly with me lately, Kate. I have been sitting by my window to-night in the moonlight, striving to get away
from myself,—resolving to take my life in my own hands and shape
it to suit my designs. In the midst of such thoughts comes these
words of Owen Meredith :

                    ' By the laws
          Of a fate I can neither control nor dispute
          I am what I am ;'

and then all that is caged and bound in my nature rises in rebellion. I must find work, *work ;* that is salvation. We women live too much in our hearts. We must get out of this heart life and live in the head, if we would not suffer.

" ' What is it now ? ' you ask. I will tell you. Yesterday Rose and I, accompanied by Don Ramon and Col. Horton, went down the coast a few miles on horseback. We stopped for lunch at the house of an acquaintance, where we learned of the illness of a sister of Doña Inez, who lived near Montecito. I was anxious to make a sketch of a certain point along the coast ; so Don Ramon proposed that Col. Horton should accompany me to the desired place, while he and Rose visited his sister-in-law ; each party going directly home when the sketch was completed and the visit made.

" Don Ramon's passion for horses is remarkable, even for a Spaniard, and we were riding two of his finest specimens. Mine had been devoted to my use from my first arrival in the family. He is a perfect model of horseflesh, of a dark cream color—*pelamino*, the Spanish call it—with black mane and tail, and a black line along the back from mane to tail. He has learned to know me, and I am very much attached to him. The canter to the beach was exhilarating, and we were in the best of spirits when we arrived at the desired spot. Taking my sketching materials from their pocket at the side of my saddle, my companion fastened our horses to a tree, and we went down to the beach. He arranged my seat on a rock, and I was soon very busy. Taking a little volume of Owen Meredith's ' Lucile ' from his pocket he said :

" ' May I read to you, Mrs. Lee, while you work ? ' to which I replied :

" 'I shall be really glad to have you, Col. Horton. " Lucile " is always a favorite with me.'

"So as I worked he read, at first continuously, then an extract here and there as he turned the leaves. It was familiar to both of us, therefore each fragment was understood. Gradually the reading became more desultory and fragmentary, interspersed between periods of silent looking out across the great waters. Then he read in a low voice this passage, descriptive of Lucile :

" ' Had her life been but blended
With some man's whose heart had her own comprehended,
All its wealth at his feet would have lavishly thrown.
For *him* she had then been ambitious alone ;
For him had aspired ; in him had transfused
All the gladness and grace of her nature ; and used
For him only the spells of its delicate power.'

" Something in the tone of voice, more in the manner of the reader, sent a sharp thrill through my heart, and made me wish I had not come to this lonely, dream-like place in this way.

" After a moment's silence he said :

" ' Men and women often accomplish great works, stung by the agony of being mis-mated ; but the best and truest work of man or woman must be from the grander stimulus of being rightly mated ; Agnes Lee, your work is from the former impulse. Would to God I could lift you out of this life to another world where you could be impelled only by the latter motive. Through all these years in which I have known you, and of you, I believe I have read your nature perfectly, all its needs, and all the purity and nobility of its impulses ; there has been an infinity of pleasure—a great danger also—

to me in the perusal. I have read the cold, unresponsive nature that would sacrifice all the grace and sweetness of your womanhood to utilitarian and mercenary uses, and the knowledge has stung me to agony. To me you are a queen amongst women. I could snatch you from this existence, though my own life were the sacrifice. I could say as the Duke de Luvois did to Lucile :

> " ' 'Tis a soul that appeals
> To a soul, 'tis a heart that cries out for a heart,
> 'Tis the man you yourself have created in part,
> That implores you to sanction and save the new life
> Which he lays at your feet with this prayer.'

" He had put his hand over mine as it lay on the rock, and I had not the power to change the position. I was dizzy and faint. A wild, passionate response was ringing through my own heart, not to this man, but to his sentiments, his cry. I felt the sands slipping, slipping from beneath me. I became afraid of myself. All the pagan in my nature rose up defiant and rebellious, demanding recognition, demanding satisfaction of this fate that had made me as I am, and denied the fulfillment of all the soul's possibilities ; that, when I begged for bread, had given me a stone.

" Then a door stood wide open in my heart, and I realized this truth, that had this man before me been what no man will ever be to me here, a realization of that grand ideal that awaits me in some life beyond this,—I should have been swept away by his call, as the branch of sea-weed was carried out by the rising tide. Then also came the further knowledge, that, though I may never encounter this ideal, yet I shall never bow to a lesser god. My womanhood can never trail her white garments through the mire of sensuality in any form, or kneel at a less worthy shrine than that of divinest love. Welcome death—welcome starvation—rather than feed upon the husks.

"Then I was strong again, my armor intact ; strong to save my-self and him. I arose and stood before him, saying :

"'My friend, I appreciate your esteem, your respect, more than I can tell you. Nothing can ever change my life's pathway. That is best which comes to each of us, how hard soever it may seem. Let us each live for the duty we owe to life. Weak and com-monplace people may stumble and fall, and arise with the mire of the street upon their garments ; but, my friend, you and I are not weak and commonplace. Let us go home now.'

" He held my hand a moment, reverently and tenderly ; then, with a deep pathos in his voice, said, only :

"'God bless you, noblest of women ! You are always true and right. We will go home.'

" As I entered, alone, the gate of home, again I met Father An-tonio, walking among the roses. A passionate desire to touch the hem of his garment, imploring his strength, came over me, and I al-most sank to the ground. My nerves had been taxed almost beyond their strength. His kindly greeting seemed like the blast of a trum-pet calling to battle. I, unconsciously, reached my hand to him, and said :

"'Father Antonio, when a heart cries to you from out of its depths, " *Pray for me* ! " do you know and understand ? '

" He took my proffered hand just a moment, his dark eyes were grave and compassionate, as he replied, slowly,

"'I know ; I understand.'

"'That was all, Kate, but Heaven's gates seemed open, and the soft breezes of Paradise calmed my troubled soul. All day those words echo softly in my heart, like the sound of music :

"'*I know*; *I understand.*'

"Your AGNES."

PART IV.

Could I but know that in some far sweet morning
We should stand side by side,
And in that hour find all Life's questions answered,
I would be satisfied.

"SANTA BARBARA, Sept. 30th.

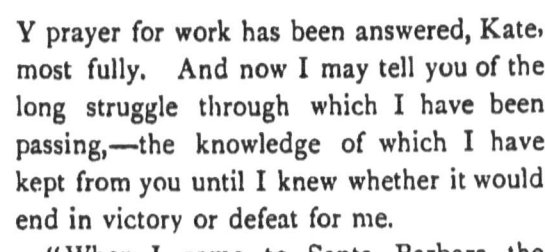

Y prayer for work has been answered, Kate, most fully. And now I may tell you of the long struggle through which I have been passing,—the knowledge of which I have kept from you until I knew whether it would end in victory or defeat for me.

"When I came to Santa Barbara the conviction was strong within me, that henceforth I must fight alone the battle of life for myself and the dear children. Not very long after my arrival here, a letter from their father confirmed this impression. He had made arrangements to remain permanently in China, and—well, Kate, there is no use calling up any ghosts by going into sad details. The bare facts are these: I have my precious babies—for which privilege I thank God every hour—my worldly possessions are not burdensome, but I am strong and brave in spirit to work for my children; and I have some talents that can be utilized in the line of teaching.

" All the facts I put before my kind friends, Doña Inez and her noble hearted husband. Their home was offered me for mine with an earnestness and warmth that admitted no refusal. They insisted that if I *would* teach, my coming here was a dispensation of

Providence in their behalf. 'Were there not all the *muchachitos* and *muchachitas* suffering for lack of instruction? Did they not need lessons in English, and music and painting, and was there a more competent person in all the Californias that *nuestra hermana querida* Agnes?' exclaimed the dear, kind Doña, folding me in a genuine Spanish embrace. I could not doubt the sincerity of their expressions. In conclusion they positively forbade me to, think of any other place than their *casa* as the home of myself and children. So that part was settled greatly to my satisfaction. A commodious school-room was fitted up in their house, and devoted to my use. Gradually numerous nieces and nephews and cousins, and other juvenile relatives of these kind friends were added to my classes, the privilege of my instruction always being solicited as a favor, until I became the centre of the busiest little hive of workers in all Santa Barbara. The remuneration which I have been compelled to take for this is really beyond my most sanguine expectations. They all insist that I must not think of leaving Santa Barbara, must establish a permanent institution here, and much more that is very pleasant for me to hear. So, with the aid of Don Ramon, arrangements were completed by which I have for a school-room a pretty little building owned by him, situated a short distance from the residence; and yesterday my school was opened for pupils with due formality. I have promised to continue the school for a year at least, and probably longer. And, Kate, I began to feel to-day for the first time that I am standing upon a solid foundation of my own. I feel an infinite capacity for work in my nature. It is a very interesting work to me, as Spanish children are always well trained, obedient and loving.

" To-day, for the first time, I feel like telling you my true position

which may possibly make clear to you some things in my former
letters that may have been somewhat obscure.

"Mrs. Howard sailed last week for New York, while Howard
remained in San Francisco. I think it is tacitly understood between
them that it is a final separation. The day before they went away, I
was at their house nearly all day, aiding her in the last preparations
for departure. It was a very sad day to both of them. Every spot
was sacred with mementoes of the little girls. A scrap of faded
ribbon that had once tied Jennie's hair, a broken doll that was
Maud's favorite, a little worn shoe in a closet, the dainty dresses in
which the mother was wont to array them with so much pride, and
which were now folded away with bitter tears ; all these things were
like daggers to the hearts of both parents.

"As I walked home in the evening, Howard went with me to my
own gate. Just before separating, he said to me :

"'Mrs. Lee, Jennie has told me that she opened her heart to you
freely. It will not be necessary for me to say anything more to you ;
I think she feels there is no longer the shadow of a reason for our
remaining together. I believe she desires to go away for a final
separation. Believe me, I shall be just and honorable with her. I
could not do otherwise, not even to hasten the hour that will bring
me, a free man, to the sweet woman, who through sorrow, and suffering, and death, must be forever the queen of my life. Strange as
it may seem to you to hear me say it, my feeling for *her* is the one
love of my strong manhood, the sweet fountain whose pure waters
have been to my soul as the baptism of God. I want you to understand me, that I am a better man in every way for this feeling. It
has changed and purified my nature, and, despite all the conditions,

I thank Heaven for having known it. I ask you to be a sister to her, Mrs. Lee. You will be her constant companion. I know you love her, and will cherish her happiness. Some day, I shall come to her, and when I do, you will approve of my coming.'

"With that he wrung my hand in farewell.

" What a strange web of the irregular and the unconventional has been woven around this place in the incidents of the past few weeks ! The events of sober, real life are often more incredible than the creations of fiction.

" Rose is paler and more quiet in her manner than before this spiritual cyclone, but otherwise she is her old sweet self. We never speak upon *the one* subject, but a mutual pressure of our clasped hands, or the interchange of eloquent glances at times, reveal to each the sympathy and understanding of the other. I am sure no one beside ourselves suspects the condition of affairs.

" Col. Horton went to Los Angeles two or three days after my last letter to you. He has interests there that may keep him permanently. He was very kind, very chivalrous and very respectful in his manner to me all the time.

" Father Antonio I meet frequently, as he is an inmate of our household. He refers occasionally to his return to Spain, which elicits most earnest protestation from every member of our family. He is a constant study to me, Kate ; he seems so different from any other man I ever knew. I wonder if he suspects the peculiar influence he has upon me, which is a most singular psychological phenomenon, and one entirely new to me. A subtle something—shall I call it soul-emanation ?—seems to surround me from his spirit, until there are hours and days in which I live and move and have my being only in this atmosphere. It is as though I were walking in the clearer ether of great mountain heights. I am uplifted and exalted until I feel that fire and torture and martyrdom could not disturb my serenity. I seem to have known him since the first dawn of creation, more intimately than I have ever known any other embodied spirit. It never appears necessary that I should speak my thoughts to him : I fancy he reads my soul as an open scroll. There is not an hour of the day in which I do not feel his presence, the benediction of his hand, the inspiration of his glance. And yet, dear, only the words of formal courtesy are ever exchanged between us. He has been a help, a power to me in these desolate hours I have known lately, greater, perhaps, than he can ever know. I imagine mine are the feelings which weak mortals feel toward the saints in heaven. But it is all new to your AGNES."

After this the letters for many weeks were filled with descriptions, of her daily routine, incidents in the lives of her idolized children, and little pen sketches of her surroundings. At last I come to this one :

JANUARY 12TH.

" Kate, can you imagine yourself closing your eyes upon a certain scene, and opening them to find every particular of that scene completely changed? Can you picture one walking along a monotonous little pathway which promises to continue indefinitely, and suddenly finding the road stopped abruptly by a great fathomless abyss which reveals only mysterious obscurity? So has Life revealed itself to me,—suddenly, as a lightning-stroke. I wonder if I can give you any clear idea of my meaning, by sober details? Let me try:

" During my vacation, which commenced about the middle of December, Don Ramon invited me with Rose, Father Antonio and some other members of his family to accompany him to his extensive ranch, which lies about forty miles from Santa Barbara, almost entirely in the mountains. He goes there frequently upon matters of business, and he was anxious to make this trip a pleasant affair in honor of his brother who will soon return to Spain.

"They arranged the trip, for my sake, in the vacation, as Doña Inez insisted that I needed the recreation. Heavy rains had fallen in the mountains, and it was not without some misgivings that we undertook the journey. But we arrived without any unpleasant incident, and were soon comfortably domiciled for a week's stay in the quaint old *adobe* farm-house, which was in charge of a Mexican family. The gentlemen spent many hours each day in the saddle, and sometimes Rose and I were their companions. But my delight was the wonderful mountain scenery on every hand. One especial rocky gorge I was fond of visiting frequently for sketching purposes. It was peculiarly located, being but a narrow box-like ravine in one portion, through which a little stream trickled, and upon each side of which the mountains rose up almost perpendicularly. In order to reach the point from which I desired to sketch, a mile or so from the house, it was necessary to pass through this narrow gorge by the merest thread of a pathway which lay along the edge of the stream. Rose and I had been to the spot many times, and I was quite familiar with the way.

" One afternoon, just before we were to take our departure from the ranch, I was quite desirous of visiting the place to complete my last sketch of an interesting waterfall. Rose was feeling quite unwell, so I took my sketch-book and went alone without the least hesitation. The work required more time than I at first anticipated, and just as I was closing my book I was surprised by falling rain-drops. Glancing up I became seriously alarmed at the appearance of the sky. The whole northern heavens seemed a black vault that threatened to engulf the earth. It was singularly grand and majestic, but I was too much frightened to admire it. Hastening my steps through the falling rain, I had but reached the narrow gorge when darkness seemed to close me in as the walls of a prison. Reverberations of thunder and flashes of lightning added to the terror of the scene. Despite my fear I remembered the description in 'Lucile,' beginning :

' And the storm was abroad in the mountains.'

" I entered the gorge—picking my way as carefully as I could, when a low moan far up the mountain attracted my attention. So faintly it came at first, that I scarcely noticed it, but gradually it grew deeper and more distinct until I paused to listen. I was standing midway in the gorge, at the time. The little stream was swollen considerably and ran over my feet. The mysterious roar became almost deafening. I knew not what to do. At this instant a bright flash of lightning revealed just before me the form of Father Antonio hastening towards me. Without an instant of waiting or word of warning he caught me in his arms and sprang like an athlete through a providential opening in the wall of the ravine, which led to a sheltered place about thirty feet above the stream. It was not an instant too soon. We had barely reached the place of safety, when I caught the gleam of a white, electric wall of water and in a moment our placid, little stream was a boiling cauldron, twenty feet in depth. There had been a cloud-burst in the mountains, and this was the result. This man had simply saved me from a most horrible death. I grew dizzy with a realization of the situation, and for a moment all consciousness forsook me. In that moment, dear, the old *I* died forever. When complete consciousness came back to me the whole universe was changed, with the rapidity and fierceness of the lightning darts that played around the rock upon which we stood. I was aroused by hearing my name, '*Agnes*.' That was all ; but the word seemed a signal that rolled away a great curtain from my soul, and I saw that revealed which I thought could never be shown to me until Time should be no more. I knew, with a knowledge as fixed as Eternity, that the deepest love of which my nature was capable, was given to this man,—that is Antonio Carillo was realized the grandest ideal possible to my soul's conception ; knew also that, even were it possible that he could ever give me a thought beyond what was given to any friend, there lay between us a gulf as broad as God's universe, as impassable as the walls of fate. With one second of time this knowledge came to me. And yet the moment in which I lay in helpless consciousness in his arms was to me an infinity of joy—the life of centuries condensed into a single instant—the epitome of eternity.'

" By the glare of the lightning I could see distinctly every outline of his face, the contour of his head, as the storm played around us. He held me firmly and closely, for the place of our shelter was small and by no means sure. He spoke no word to me, but gazed into the face of the tempest with an air of reverent admiration, as though in it he recognized and adored the Omnipotent.

"For one wild moment I closed my eyes and prayed for instant death. I begged the storm to absorb my being, the lightning to extinguish with one kind stroke the pitiful torch of life. Only for a moment. Then, like a great, calm river, there came to me from this man a peace, deep and abiding. I was lifted above the spiritual storm and placed upon heights which seething waves of earthly unrest can never reach. I believe for a time my spirit was free from the body, and stood revealed to his as it will be when earthly things are put aside forever. Like the faint sound of distant music came the memory of his words upon another occasion long ago—'*I know; I understand.*' In that moment I bowed my head to a Hand that consecrated me, for this life, to a work in which I must never feel the sense of sacrifice ; in which I must feel that the complete satisfaction of the reward that will come to me in the life beyond will be sufficient for any loss that could be possible on earth.

"Then the storm died away as rapidly as it had come. The great black clouds rolled slowly back and the full moon was revealed, shining as placidly as though material or spiritual tempests were unknown. Then he arose, his arm still supporting my trembling form, and thus we made our way through the gorge and across its stream which had returned almost to its usual insignificance.

"At the doorway of the house he clasped my hand firmly and kindly for a brief instant, then saying only, ' May God bless you, he turned away and went out into the night, alone.

"Through the long night I did not close my eyes,-—I lived an eternity. In the morning he had returned to Santa Barbara, whither we all went the same day.

"This morning he sailed for San Francisco on his way to Spain. With a brief word of farewell to me he placed in my hand a little cluster of violets all wet with rain-drops. I pinned them on my breast, where they are resting now. I have sat here by my window all day bravely struggling with a part of my nature that I must henceforth hold in check with the firm hand of a master. All day I have realized only this, that I shall never see him again in this life. The clasping of his kindly hand must be to me but a memory henceforth. Even should I meet him it must be with the quiet exterior of a passing acquaintance. And yet,—oh, Kate! Kate! with my soul strung to an agony of consciousness, I know that at one word from him,— at one glance of his eyes, the floodgates would be swept away and I could no more stay the passionate surges of this feeling that possesses me, than I could check the seething torrent of Vesuvius. Did I hear his voice calling me, did I feel the magnetic attraction of his presence desiring me, I should go to him, though from Heaven to Hell. I could not stand alone against the invitation of his hand. I am not ashamed to tell you this, Kate. There is nothing in my heart that I would not lay before the Mother of God. This feeling is so exalted, so ennobling, that it places me beyond the reach of earthly temptation. I can never walk alone, though I tread the wilderness of sorrow; for, though I shall never see him in earth-life, yet, strange incongruity, I can never lose his presence from my side. He kneels beside me at every altar; he stands by my side on the lonely sea shore, when the voice of God speaks from His ocean; his spirit-hand responds to the yearning pressure of my own in every scene that thrills my soul with joy or sorrow ; his eloquent glance will go with me through eternity.

" Every pure, noble desire of my nature responds to this man, as a harp to the hand of a master. Every act of his—the strong, quiet grace of his movements—the dignity of his language—the almost haughtiness of his bearing—are to me the perfection of harmony, the music of existence. Until this revelation came to me, I could not have conceived the possibility of one human being fulfilling so completely the highest ideal of another, as he does to me.

" All these things stand out in my soul with a distinctness that is torture, as I sit here amid the roses of Santa Barbara, and feel that every pulsation of Time bears him farther from me—away from me forever. And I ask of Fate, Why has this experience come to me ? Why have I been called to antedate Eternity, and stand hand-clasped with that which should have come to me in the Life beyond this ? To-morrow I must take up the burden of life again ! Oh, my beloved, pray for me !   AGNES."

After this, in all the letters that came from her, this one subject was never mentioned. Her life was very full of work. The months glided by, until a year had passed since the date of this last letter. Then came a long one, telling of Howard's coming back. A quiet divorce had been granted, and both parties to this singular union were free. Jennie had been reunited to her old lover, Victor Ellerton, soon after the divorce. And now this long letter from Agnes described the marriage of Rose and Howard, and their departure for their new home in San Francisco. During the year, the graves of the two little girls had been tenderly cared for by Rose ; and before the final departure for their new home, she had knelt with the father by the cherished mounds.

The years wore on, and Paul and Mary needed greater educational advantages than could be obtained in Santa Barbara. The death of a relative left Agnes in a much better financial condition than before. She was able to fulfill her dream of a trip to Italy with her children, where she remained some years, until they were little ones no longer, but a manly lad and winsome lass, who were as devoted to their 'precious mamma,' as the most loving heart could desire. Then they returned to San Francisco, where she found her beloved Rose grown a sweet, matronly woman, wearing most gracefully her crown of maternity; and Howard very happy, with his handsome boys and girls, while his love for his wife had but gained strength and tenderness with the flight of the happy years of their married life.

Then came rumors of the terrible ravages of cholera in Spain, and long accounts of the noble conduct of one whose name was a household word to the sorrowing and afflicted, not alone in his native city, but beyond its walls—Antonio Carillo. At last came a day when this grand soldier in the noble army of God put off his armor, and responded to the summons of the Master whom he had served so gloriously.

After this the hold of life seemed weakened with her; and one sweet June day she folded her patient hands across her pure heart in the eternal rest, and her sorrowing children laid her tenderly by the side of the little baby that died so many years before. Their father never returned to them, nor communicated with them. Before her death she asked Mary to send me a package of papers, among which I found this poem, bearing date some years after the eventful parting at Santa Barbara :

UN SUEÑO DE LA NOCHE.

You decked my breast with violets last night, —
    Their haunting sweetness thrills my pulses yet ;
You clasped my eager hands with warm caress,
    And kissed the sadness from my eyelids wet.

My soul is sad at memory of your touch,
    Your flowers' rich fragrance thrills my heart with pain ;
The look of pitying kindness in your eyes
    May never come to gladden me again.

For, all the sweetness of that haunting scene—
    Your thrilling touch—your violets' purple gleam—
The glance of kindness from your speaking eyes—
    Were but the offspring of a strange, sweet dream.

I wake—to know your hand can ne'er clasp mine
    This side of life—this side of Hope and Heaven,—
To know that not one kindly glance of yours
    Must ever to my longing eyes be given.

I wake—to take my burden up again,
    Forget for one sweet hour of dreaming night,—
My weary burden of the heart and brain—
    And do my duty with my woman's might.

I would not look upon your face again—
    Your strong, grand face that is a god's to me—
I would not hear the music of your voice,
    I would not think of you, or hear or see

One spoken, written word that could recall
   Your memory. For only thus to me
Can come a strength to do my daily work
   For which my spirit must be brave and free.

You came into my life for one brief hour,
   Strong, noble, grand as any god could be ;
And all the currents of my being's tide—
   And life itself, henceforth were changed to me.

You came—and passed. Now never more to me
   Can come the clasping of your firm, true hand,
Must shine the glory of your eloquent eyes,—
   No more to me, this side the Heavenly Land.

I pray for strength. I would be firm and brave
   To put your very memory away ;
I pray for strength, and it is granted me
   To meet the burdens of the toilful day.

But in the dreaming mystery of Night
   Such visions come sometimes of bliss and pain,
That with the dawning of another day
   The hard-won battle must be fought again.

And yet—until the soul shall pass the bridge
   That spans the mystic gulf from shore to shore,
There must remain between my soul and yours
   The eloquence of silence—evermore.